Infatuation, Love, And Heartbreak
A Book of Poems

Briana Isham

Father, thank you for the life lessons in
infatuation, love, and heartbreak.

Contents

Opened Faith

Having another person in your life to open
your eyes and given butterflies,
That person you just don't want to lose but something went wrong,
And it all ended sad but true,
But the fact that they are still in your life,
It's something that is still true though from
time to time you see yourself thinking,
"Damn, why I ever let you go?"

But time changes things even when the world sees differently.
There comes a time when life gets hard and you start asking yourself,
"Where the heck I went wrong?"
That time, when you just want things to go back the way they were,
Before things got hard,
It's easier to float on air when things weren't so complicated.

But hey, life gives you lemons —
That's the time to make lemonade.
The older you get the more lemons you will catch.
Never fall from God because God never leaves your side.

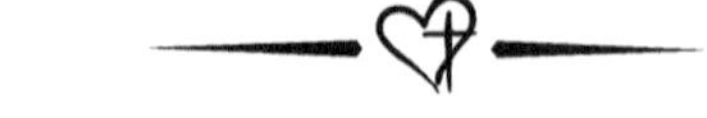

Not Settling For Less

Why should I settle for less?
When I know my worth?
I'm a princess turning into a queen,
Ready to find my prince soon to be a king.

Never the other way around —
Never a princess to a peasant,
Never a prince to a frog,
But for all the riches in the world,
I would never let him fall.
But why should I settle for something less than I deserve?

When I know my worth,
And where I come from,
Only the best, never less.
I know what I'm used to,
Me getting my way,
But what I deserve is to be happy in every way,
Something to think about,
When trying to come my way.

Always thinking of others before putting yourself carrying it is,
But time for a rest.
Take care of yourself,
You are young; live for now and be free.

Life brings troubles,
Life brings happiest,
Also brings discouragement,
But to overcome it all is a blessing in its self.
Just live and be free,
Never settle for less.

Shame

Do you see what happened?
You broke my heart, crushed my spirit,
And get mad at me when I stop caring,
For all feelings doesn't matter,
Because that day you broke my heart.

This woman who had a heart full of gold,
Became a woman with a heart cold as ice.
Never seeing that he could be a good guy,
Probably let a good guy pass me by.

But that doesn't stop me,
For I'm a very independent soul, you see,
Looking for someone to who can take the cold,
With just a simple touch could warm the soul.

Not asking for much but someone to love,
When you simply just want to give up on love.
Is that too much to ask for simple love in return?
They say it's better to have loved than lost,
But hey, getting hurt by another is just something I can live without.

The guy isn't always at fault,
But in this situation, he just copped out.
But we gone switch sides for now,
Because I'm not bitter, I'm just speaking my mind.
Now a guy goes to say that he wants true love,
But what is truly love?

If this generation keeps being at war,
Keeps downing, hurting, and promising lies to one another,
But then turns around and wants to be loved by another,

Is a twisted fantasy, you see!
We're going to continue to be at war with each other,
Because everyone's playing a game and everyone seems to be losing.
It's just a DAMN Shame!

Infatuation, Love, And Heartbreak: A Book of Poems

Is a twisted fantasy, you see!
We're going to continue to be at war with each other,
Because everyone's playing a game and everyone seems to be losing.
It's just a DAMN Shame!

Wishing

Wishing and hoping for a new tomorrow,
Lord knows all anyone wants is that "good ole" tight hug,
But at the end of the day, we must hold ourselves,
Tell ourselves that everything will be OK. I swear,
I never thought a day would come when I looked in the mirror,
I had nothing to say,
But Jesus, take my hand, guide me to the light.

Let me see what I have missed, but I have feared about that dream,
I had when I all I could see was dark from hell.
I was on a slippery slope of no return when I remembered,
I must have faith and believe in you.

Oh lord, for thou has been there from the beginning,
And won't leave, not even in the end.
But all I can see is the little girl's face looking at me in the mirror,
Saying, "Why did you give up on our sweet life?
We're all we had but you forgot about me,
And now I'm lost here on this cold edge,
Wishing you would remember this little girl you left for dead.
Dreaming that my world could change, I'm here to say to you,
Congratulations for all the pain.

You overcame and for coming back to rescue
me from this cold, cold, hell,
It's a new beginning for us now, let's live it well.
Believe and have faith that your world
Is better than ever, my dear.
We have not left you nor forsaken you —
You will always be in my heart reminding me,
Not to leave left for dead.

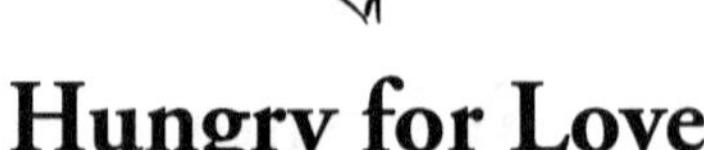

Hungry for Love

Hungry for love and affection,
Something life-changing,
A world where everyone can love,
No hurt in the eyes of others.
Why only hurt?

When they say it's better to have loved than lost,
I can't say I agree.
I would rather not lose the fight for love,
But so few feels that way.
But love is a special thing,
Shared by two people.

Why misunderstand?
What's real and there?
Why mistreat and abuse the ones who care?
Although we as humans only care for ourselves,
It's just not fair.

Living in sin,
A lifeless life to live,
Wish we could go back in time.
Things may have made more sense then
Than waiting for Mr. or Ms. Right.
Move on and live life just as everyone else,
With only yourself in sight.

A Happy Dream

What they said was a dream,
I just couldn't believe,
Because in the end,
There you were standing with life.
I couldn't believe my eyes.
Was it you there by the window?
Gazing out at the stars,
I had to close my eyes,
Thought twice it couldn't be.
Yet, I closed my eyes and reopened them and it was true,
No one other but you.
All I wanted to do was scream,
But I just cried and threw out a big hug.
With grace I was happy to see you, although scared.
I couldn't seem to bring myself to end such a happy dream.

An Unfinished Love

Gave you too much,
Let me slip through the cracks.
Now he's saying he really need this,
But every chain reaction has a flaw.

That is the day we all know the truth,
Reactions may be a happy ending,
But it never seems to fail and is always in
some kind a way, happy or sad.
Well, here in the same, come witness the truth.
Read in between the lines, see the face to face you never knew.

This is the time when one noticed a woman,
With some brains to the sacrifice of love.
Discontinued me you never know I know,
The truth of the love that was there between the eyes.

Working

Working to gain a pay,
Working hard to gain a life,
Working hard for love that will never show,
Working hard to please others but why?
No need to work for nothing but life.
We are who we set out to be,
Be whatever it is you please.
Forget the users,
Forget the actors,
Let go of the damage in life.
Be blessed and rest,
Behold the rest of life,
Today is the day we all see the meaning.

Butterflies

O sweet butterflies,
You filled my heart,
With such sweet delight.
Sun rays are shining,
A fulfilling moment in life.
Shining the rays never felt so great,
The gray areas fade away.

O sweet butterflies,
Filing such a cold heart,
Iced over in deep water,
Sweet butterflies, never leave my side.
With you and only you,
You brought me out this drought,
O sweet butterflies.

Started To Care

Started to care for someone who doesn't;
Caring leads to nothing but feelings,
Pain, lust, and a heart full of hurt.

A thought of something but nothing —
Caring for nothing,
Makes a heart cold,
A person colder.

Love and caring have no place holder,
A fight for something or a fight for importance.
It's not that important,
If it's not worth fighting for.

I love,
I like,
I see
What I want.
I go after, I fight, I get.
I want nothing,
But love, happiness, and peace.
A life worth living,
Is something great?
Achieve nothing but greatness.

Family

Family sweet and true,
No love is just not true,
Bad or good,
The struggles we get through.
What can you say?

Other than live for you,
Family is here to stay.
People come and go.
It's 2014, people screaming, New Year, new me!
But never change.
When does it end?

When are individuals,
Actually going to change to better themselves?
I say it's a good question,
But uh,
Some people have it to change for the better,
And, well, others have no set goals.

A Young Black Female

Is strong in who she is?
Independent as can be,
Never wrong in the game,
She turns all the hurt into gain.

So-called, becomes an angry black female,
But don't complain,
Because you made her this way.
Don't bash her because you gave her more strength,
You would ever know.

Can't imagine how strong she has become,
A young black female,
Ambidextrous in her dealings,
Can't seem to tell her nothing,
Yet she is a strong black female.

Single as can be,
Can't trust easily,
But as a black male they can't see why
She's as strong,
Being a single black female,
 Not in need of any man.

To help her obtain anything,
She got where she is today by God and her strength.
Let him not think,
It was because he was with her,
Because she is a,
Young black female!

I want

I want that kind of love,
That makes you want to be together every moment of the day,
That kind of love that can't go a day without hearing their voice,
You want to be the first and last person they speak to.

When you just want to stay on the phone
and listen to each other breathe,
The kind of love that stay in the honeymoon phase,
Where you want to be all up under each other,
That kind of love in which you don't get tired of a person,
That kind of love you just want to show off to the world,
That kind of love you can't go a day without,
That kind of love you only desire to spend
the whole day doing nothing,
Yes…that kind of love!

The Substance

That thing you so dearly love,
That frees your mind and cools your soul,
To escape from the things you just can't seem to handle,
Running straight to the bottle, the air guiding you to the clouds,
You can't escape this fear of life for eternity.

When you return from this vacation,
The more you realize you're back in that same situation,
Not knowing that there's more to life,
Than running back to that moment of relaxation,
The only thing that matters is that drunken moment of being dazed,
The fear of life has dread away.

Now going to the smoke to lose your mind,
Being on cloud nine,
Made you forget the worries for that moment in time.
Now back to reality where you are face-to-face
with that fear you wanted to leave behind?
Screaming damn, if only these moments could last a life time,
Once again, running back to that substance
you just think is oh so fine!

Disturbing Feeling

This disturbing feeling,
It's taking control of my mind,
Have me second guessing life?

The world is spinning and I'm standing still,
Not making a sound,
But there is a sound,
Whether you hear it or not.

Feeling as if no one truly cares,
Outside of family there's an alone feeling,
But I try to be strong but deep down my soul is hurting,
Crying out, but no one hears those sweet, sweet, cries of damnation,
Thoughts going crazy.

My mind is a dangerous place at times,
You can't begin to imagine,
Understand nothing I'm saying,
If I tried you would worry,
First question would be, "Are you suicidal?"
I thought about it,
Only wishing those words never cross my lips,
You wouldn't understand me if I said it.

First thing to your mind is, "We need to get her help."
I don't need help, I need to break free of my shackles;
I'm a danger to myself.
Knowing that the world is full of opportunities,
My opportunities feel like failures.

Feel like I wasted my life trying,

Trying to achieve or become something I would
or could never obtain or even do,
But in my heart, I'm strong.
Can never be taken down by my own dangerous thoughts,
Only if you knew what's deep inside my mind and soul,
All you would say is, "The child needs serious attention or help,"
But in reality, all I want is family, and a love of my life,
But that's just in fairytales.

Lost In Thought

Mind at a blank,
Gone with the wind,
The flow is controlled,
Blowing in different directions.
What's to come?

Must stay in control.
What has happened?
Have lost my way in the world,
So much to be done.

Starting over,
Is just a new.
Ha, you don't know,
Lost in space, in mind, in sight —
Best of all lost in might.

Loving the night,
All dried up the sun burned out,
Don't know what's going on.
It's funny you know,
I'm always in control,
Lost in thought.

A Drifted Passion

The world it may change,
Say the same thing each day,
Don't know how to feel,
My word sounds the light is darker,
Waiting for a new light.

Come take me away from the pain.
It's not you, it's me.
Although the words may sting,
It's true,
Don't cry out for a love you will not obtain,
Living in sin,
What more do I want?

I'm losing myself,
In the words,
In the sights.
It's crazy how much time changes.
Can we go back to the old days where?
Chivalry never died.

The lost hope of a generation,
The lost hope of self,
I see a drifting soul of passion.
It's gone closed off from you,
You obtain It somehow.

Gaining access to a deep hole,
I left for dead in the back of my mind,
Though my thoughts cry out through my expressions,
Seeing beneath my cries,
How should I feel?
Lost in mind.

Always Smiling

A faded smile,
A crushing laugh,
Why care?
The actions never there,
It's a shame I swear.

It's crazy these things.
The sky is dark,
But you smile.
How is this so?
Why do you smile?

A smile that lights up the room,
Not knowing what's truly there,
But a smile can hide it all,
What is true anymore?
What is there is never there,
Though I'm happy.

Deep down I feel some kind of way,
Love go first,
Love me always,
Forever a loner,
Always smiling!

I'm All That Matters

Wanting to rip you out and toss you away,
Stop controlling I will, just throw you away,
Luckily, I need you to live.

I'm abandoning you,
Leaving you in the dust,
Don't want this Burden.
It just sucks.

Why must I succumb to your lust for life?
It's apparent that you're a useless factor,
Just a mind-controlling factor.

The heart had no play.
It just pumps the blood going around only for life.
Start controlling your mind.
Forget the thoughts; it's all a moment in time I guess.
Why stress over the things no one truly cares for?

Being nice, even to nice,
Will someday end you in a world of trouble.
No matter it's just that — a mind thing.
That's all that matters.

Situational Sensation

Drunken sensation,
Awesome word play,
Lustful thinking going array,
Wanting that sensation
Only for the moments.
Everlasting company,
Only to get out that quick sensational opportunity,
Making yourself ease,
Your mind convinced it's fair, it's alright,
Knowing in your mind is just the moments,
Everlasting moments of sensation.

Emotional Wall

Drops and falls,
Who cares?
That thought just dropped.
Out of sight, out of mind.
No words could express that feeling.

That unspeakable feeling,
No longer caring,
A burden lifted,
What's more to say?
Other than it's just moments —
Those moments I could do without.

Thought I was out cold before;
This realization it's always colder somewhere else,
So done with this business,
What's the point?
It was started with low expectations of failure.

The truth of its worth,
Was known from the start,
So why was it started in the beginning?
That's the question in sight,
Though emotional walls dropped,
It just so happens to build up right.

Hopeless Romantic

No, not me,
The love of another,
Yes, I would like,
It's not a must,
Just something I want,
Thought could live without.

I love hard,
Simple as that,
But emotionless is how I'll try to react.
Don't go too deep with emotions,
Most never last,
Or maybe they're just the moments never lasting.

Go to tell a story,
Eyes all glossy,
Screaming with joy,
Happy to see your face,
The joy of being with you.
Don't care the length,
Don't know if it's true,
But in this moment,
I've saw the light.

Hopeless in love with the thoughts,
Not there in love yet,
Regardless of intense passion,
There is a true light,
Let's just say,
The light hasn't found us yet.

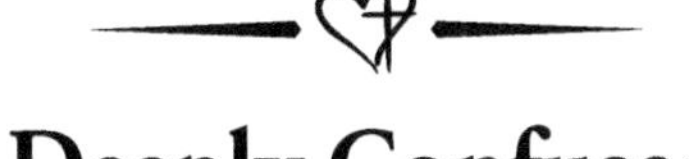

Deeply Confused

Only time could tell the paths,
The future is untold,
Hold deeply confused,
Only thoughts are flowing.

I'm a little girl lost on this road,
So lost I can't imagine,
How I found my way,
Down this path of no redemption;
It's a lonely road.

I must tell you,
This seems to happen,
Often as I could tell you.
Don't know how to feel,
So wrapped in emotions,
Should I run and hide?

Just want to cry,
Let the world see my tears,
Go on and follow.
Don't give me what you think I want,
If it's not what you want,
Call it what it is.

A fling in the end,
Don't know how to feel,
Emotionally drained,
Don't want to go through it,
Just adding more emotions to the fire.

Crying out in pain,

Don't try to contain,
I gave up on it,
Not long after.
It was you that spark this candle,
I so long ago blew out,
I just don't get it.
I'm just lost,
Playing in mine field,
Deeply you try to understand.
You have yet to begin,
Deeply confused and over it.

Trying To Forget What I Feel

Only to be put back to the beginning,
The spark I felt then is still there.
Can't fight it cause you know it's there,
Being open is what I don't share.

Can't help but feel, the more I try to hide it, the more it comes out.
When I want something, I want it.
Can't have it; I want it more,
That's life, everybody is the same in that matter,
But in all, all I can do is just say, God will show us the way.
I feel for you, that much of this friendship is great,
Only thing is, it feels more than just that.

------ ❦ ------

The First Day We Meet

I felt a spark,
You intrigue me,
Your thoughts, your actions, your words,
Just being you, all surprised me.

Yet, I haven't fallen hard,
I accept how I feel,
Trying to hide thoughts that shouldn't be spoken,
I seem to spill what's on my mind,
Trying to hide emotions by my will, I can't
make myself do it with you.

Thoughts running wild,
Mind wanting to connect with your mind,
Nothing other than that matters,
Just our minds connecting together
Is what drives the ambition of this thing I feel.

My emotions running wild,
To allow myself to give in to them is breath-
taking, but I like it; it's wild and crazy,
The intensity of a kiss that was wild,
From then I knew that it was something,
That couldn't, shouldn't have happened,
But I liked it and if the day was to start over, I would do it all over.

I feel as though it all was right,
No wrong was done,
But it was.
If only that wasn't the case,
I would just tell you everything and anything,
But right now, I won't;

This feeling I feel is great.

Can't help but to just blush and smile,
I want you want to be in my life,
Something more than friends,
But I'm trying to hide that simple fact.

35

Being Used And Abused
For His Own Pleasure

How would he feel if we played him?
Degraded him, killed his spirit,
Crushed his heart; little does he know,
The ones who been hurt,
Know the game.

We can smell that mess a mile away,
Tries to manipulate,
Get inside her head,
Heart as cold as ice,
Feeling like there is no being nice.

Can't steal a person's happiness for your own pleasure,
Can't stand those individuals who drive me mad,
Swear they care, selfish bastards,
Only thinking of self-feelings,
Emotions don't matter,
In a world filled with selfish individuals,
Being used and abused.

If I Knew Then What I Know Now

Things would be different,
Would be no hurt in my heart,
Less mistakes,
Started business adventure early,
No guys,
Less drama,
Less stress.
If I knew then what I know now,
Would have treated you better,
Wouldn't have taken love for granted,
Less emotional drama,
Less fighting myself,
With those emotions,
Allowing them to flow—
If I knew then what I know now.

Something To Get Off My Mind

Just a thought,
A sight to see,
You are beauty, handsome as can be.
Never wanted this,
Take it back.
Feelings rushing wild,
Emotions you will never see,
Tears forming,
I hate caring,
Hate putting my heart on the line.

When all everyone does is stump holes right through it.
See, you would never understand,
Why this wasn't supposed to happen.
Yet, it did, now,
I blame myself,
For allowing this to happen.

If only words could express what it is I was feeling,
Maybe then you could understand,
On the outside looking in, I look sad,
When all there is happiness,
Only thing seen is that feelings that shouldn't be are and there alone.

You May Want To Understand

Doesn't mean you will;
You say you understand,
I don't think you do.
Those words you say,
It may touch a soul,
Regardless of how,
It made someone's day.

Though I can't relate,
I see the world differently;
There's something in you,
I have yet to figure out why,
All I can say is I do,
But those words I can't release.

Why/how did I allow this to go through?
Should have kept the distance I set.
I said I would never,
Get lost in that,
It just may so happen,
I can't relate.

Life is too short to hold things back,
Unless you're not there I'll say that.
The truth is the truth,
Just come to sorts with that;
I'm sorry, I just can't relate.

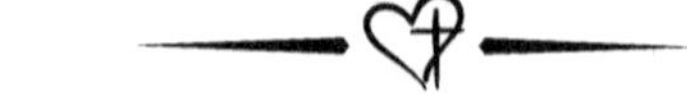

Don't Underestimate

An understanding could go a long way;
To understand the soul is another story,
Getting deep within,
Taking the time to learn and teach each other,
To be one with each other.

The story is ...
Well, it's not a story at all.
The sun it shines for a new day,
The moon is simply a nice-looking star,
But what are we in the end,
Other than a couple of cute little kids?

Wandering in the fields,
A hopeless romantic I might be,
A loner till death I can be,
Not waiting on a soul,
I am in control.

This is me against the world,
Fighting for what I want,
Rather it's love or maybe just stability;
The point is I want love,
Not hoping for it,
It really doesn't matter.

All in all, we're just poor people living in a rich man's land,
Trying to find ourselves,
Trying to succeed.
Although we can do it,
It's still a hard task indeed,
Getting through the motions and moments,

Rolling with life the best way we can.
All we want is someone to understand.

Rolling with life the best way we can.
All we want is someone to understand.

The Only One

Since day one you were there,
Never have you left me;
You're the only one I can count on.
You're there when I'm sick,
When I'm down,
When I cry,
Whenever,
Where ever,
No matter how far or how close.

You're there,
No matter how mad, how angry,
You're there,
Not because you have to be,
But because you wanted to be.

When I'm hurting, you cheer me up,
When I need you, you're there waiting with open arms,
You're the only one forever and ever more,
My mother,
My God.
You're the only one I need,
When no one else is there,
When I'm feeling alone in the world,
There is no one but you.

What Is Love?

But pain,
A useless feeling of nothingness,
Why be consumed when the outcome is pain?
Why care when no one else does?
Why be consumed with pain, lust, and nothingness?

No room for love,
For care,
For pain,
Why care for something that isn't there?
Why love when all it does is hurt you?
Love kills family,
Leaves you alone,
Nothing but nothingness.

Ambitionless Soul

To let it all die,
What education?
What future?
Ambitionless fools,
Drama killers of a moon,
No more to give,
No more to grieve
Simply over it.

No need to speak,
The world is cold,
Go big or go home,
No need for false hope,
A useless burden to the soul.

Lost but not forgotten in sight,
Too much to gain,
Too soon to be lost,
He didn't call you yet.
Love and learn,
Forget the discouragement,
It's a new day,
Fall in place,
And make a way,
Ambitionless soul.

Moments

Everyone wants to live in moments,
Moments don't last forever.
This generation has no morals,
What do you stand for?

I feel like a stranger,
You're so close but yet so far away.
You know it all,
I remember nothing,
Damn this mind.

I'm lost, spinning out of control,
Wrapping my mind trying to remember,
Starting fresh,
A new beginning.

How could I feel so much?
But know so little?
Can't be so,
A wrecking ball of disaster.

But you're intrigued,
Trying to wrap my mind,
Why do you care so much?
Is still my main question,
Something I just can't seem to answer.

Shot In The Heart

As I got shot in my heart,
Just a little girl,
In a world full of hate,
Discouraged and amazed,
Not knowing I had a special little heart.

A tomboy but I still liked boys,
Shot in the heart,
Turned and was punched in the face,
Though your words never hurt me,
It took a toll on my heart.

I wanted to scream and to lash out,
Was hit with bricks everyday as a child,
No one knew or would ever find out.
The hurt I felt,
The shame I felt,
Even followed me,
Lost little girl.

Hated by many, loved by none,
Lost little girl pushed down,
But fought back hard,
Do you see her face?

She was either you, or you were the one shooting her every chance you got,
Hurting her, but never knowing you got through,
So, you tried again every day, just to break her spirits,
Though you never got to the core,
But has she forgotten? no,
Has she let go? no,
What does she believe other than she's strong, but forever alone?

Excitement Lost

Lost in the clouds,
Wanting to jump off,
So far at the edge,
No one could catch me.
Taking a deep fall to the surface,
No one's there to catch me.

Fallen and can't get up,
Must I continue to fight this continuous fight?
To survive,
To strive,
A fight between myself.

Can't seem to get the fight to end,
A constant reminder of unsatisfactory,
Of a million goals so far away, I can barely touch.
At the edge I turned,
To reconcile my thoughts and position.

Though life is hard,
Can't let it knock you down;
There's more in life to conquer.
It's time to conquer the world,
One step at a time.

Moments Don't Last Forever

Though it was fun while it lasted,
It was wrong in the making,
Went too far too fast,
Now we're waiting.

Trying to find the words, the path to be taken,
Though I knew it would go nowhere, no how,
I liked the feeling,
Don't care of the measure,
It happened.
I feel the same,
It won't change,
It's not fair.

But it is what it is;
Lost for words,
Don't know where to start.
This thing we call life
Is a hard pill to swallow.

Living for the moments is for you,
Living for the future is me.
Everything has a reason and a season,
The moments don't last forever.

Can't Be Forced

Can't be forced,
Something so real,
Just at the tip of your fingers,
Simple little touch it's yours.

Though it's so close,
Doesn't mean it's yours;
Work for what you want,
Pray that it comes to you.

If it's meant to be,
Let it be.
Only God can tell.
Nothing to play with,
It's simple, not easy.

What more do you want?
To conquer the world,
It won't be easy;
Takes time and planning.
Till the end I'll be with you,
Let's just say the end never reaches.

In Love Too Soon

Fell in love with his mind,
Is that such a crime?
Only to be just a dime,
In his millions of coins.

Waiting to hear that rhyme,
A simple touch could ease my mind,
No complaints -what a wonderful time,
Can one believe the many lies?
Only to realize it was just a fun time?

Can't really be mad,
You gave into the crime —
Crime of passion,
With sweet fantasy,
Of the love that could be mad,
Though you knew the mindset.

Of course, you didn't listen to the deep set,
A setup of lust,
Of a crazy fling;
That's all it truly is,
A simple fling,
Of a deadly piece of cookie.

Watch out,
Cause nowadays,
A good heart doesn't matter;
Everyone wants that lustful,
Sensation that can possibly put you in a situation,
Though some make a crime out of a bad situation.

A Simple Frustration

Frustration of a simple kind,
Life is hard.
It goes on,
Just another day gone.

Lost in a cold, cold world,
Where no one seems to care,
Why fight so hard?
When you're losing a fight-less war?
Why care for the world?
When the world never cared?
Why even try living a lie?
What's the point anymore?

Given up on a crazy situation,
Love in my heart,
For something that doesn't matter,
Can't bear to explain,
The pain I feel of this frustration.

A simple temptation,
Of lustful sensation,
Mind blowing,
Crazy sensation.
But what's the point of hurting so much,
For something of a useless matter?

Never felt so heartless,
To bear what was felt.
Over time, it's just a wasteful temptation.

A Fight No More

My heart is a drum;
It beats to its own race,
Caught in a maze,
Lost in my own daze.

What's real anymore?
What actually matters?
Is life so hard?
You lose all control,
When you feel so knocked down,
But you can't just fall.

How deep will you travel?
To see the Great Wall?
It's big journey,
To see a great artifact.
I've lost so much,
Gained so little in time.

But again, what's real anymore?
What truly matters?
Can't give in,
Can't give up,
Have to stay strong no matter what.

I've lost the will to fight,
I gave in and gave up.
No turning back, what's done is done,
My heart is the drum.

Of no more beats strummed,
Though I must fight,

The fight must go on,
Goodbye to a little drum.

53

O What a Dream

What is a dream?
Touch the stars,
A lifted scream,
To obtain what could be reached,
To see to the heavens above.
What can you see?

Look into the storm;
I'm standing on the shore searching,
To obtain that thing I once knew.
I looked over the edge to see what you drew;
I only wished to obtain,
That love and fame.

Searching

In a black and blue state,
Spinning around,
Searching on the shore,
What can I see?
Life in the sky,
Feel my pain,
See what I see.

You have lost,
Lost the will to move in my shoes.
What have you lost other than that thing you so once willed for?
I lost that feeling,
Feeling of care,
To simply give up.
There's no more feeling inside of me.

It is lost in the wind;
You thought it was cool,
To play the fool.
Even if you thought the world was on your side,
You have lost out on something that was so good.

Glad to see in the sky,
What the world holds,
Less than what the forest fire rose.
If in a sense you thought I was dead,
I have awakened and I'm a fire burning to the core.
My heart has melted and in its spot this ice has filled.

Was It Ever?

What if I'm in trouble?
You always said you would be there,
Or was that a lie too?
Was it all just a lie?

I don't believe you ever cared —
Why should I believe you actually cared?
What makes it true?
Your words mean nothing,
Just a simple play,
Getting what you wanted all along.

What was true?
What part of it was true?
Why should I believe?
Believe your sick twisted lie,
The lie that made it worthwhile,
Was it ever any truth?

Can't Bear The Pain

Why understand this pain?
Fight through and stay sane.
I can't bear this pain,
A pain of carelessness,
Why keep fighting?

Fighting through this unbearable pain,
Sweeping through my body,
Causing the tears to rain,
What is left,
To this lifeless creation?

Pain sweeping through,
Irritating my mind,
The flow sincerity,
I've lost the will to move on.
Wanting to push on,
Why try to get out?
Can't barely move.

Something You Have Obtained Fun But True

A lost in memory,
Sad but true.
What's the point?
It's a simple waste of truth.

Love means nothing
In a game of war,
Lost at heart,
A cold sight,
A heartless matter,
Doesn't count to fight.

I've lost a feeling,
I can't bear to watch,
It's a simple loss of the heart.

Love isn't simple,
Lust is a lie,
Faithful my ass,
In a care-free life,
What's the point anymore?

Love means nothing anyhow;
It's always been a game you see.
It's the matter,
Of who will win my draw.

To a lustful soul,
A lost at love,
Forget it all.

It never mattered,
It was a lie.

Another countless affair-
Kill the light, it came too late this time.
Is everything black and grey?

59

The Waiting Game

Playing with hearts of hearts,
Caring for thoughts,
The touch of your touch,
Screaming get out.
Why the game?
Why fight?

It's a lost love,
Maybe just a lust gone wrong.
Why play a game? We're all losing.
Are we different,
Or just like everybody else?
All playing in this war with each other,
We're all players, right?
Why not play to win?

ENTEGRITY
CHOICE PUBLISHING

P.O. Box 453
Powder Springs, Georgia 30127

www.entegritypublishing.com
info@entegritypublishing.com

770.727.6517